# THE HAPPY SNOWMAN

**Contributing Writer**
Carolyn Quattrocki

**Illustrations**
Susan Spellman

Publications International, Ltd.

"It's snowing! Come look, Matt," cried Jenny. Matt ran to the window. Jenny was right! The snow was covering everything in sight.

Matt and Jenny ran to find their snow boots so that they could go to the park and play with their friends. "I want to come, too!" said Marianna. But Matt told her she was too small. Maybe she could come later.

Jenny and Matt put on their jackets and raced out the door.

Lisa, Tracy, and Paul were already at the park by the time Matt and Jenny got there. They decided to build a snowman. When they had finished, Jenny said, "He needs a face and some clothes." Everyone ran home to see what they could find.

Lisa found some bright, black pieces of coal for his eyes and a button for his nose. Tracy borrowed her big brother's purple scarf, and Paul brought a toy corncob pipe.

Matt and Jenny found an old pair of boots. But Marianna found the best thing of all, a black silk top hat! "Marianna, you can bring the hat for our snowman," said Jenny.

Back at the park, the children gave the snowman a face and dressed him up. Finally, Paul and Jenny put the silk top hat on their snowman's head.

"What shall we name him?" asked Tracy. "How about Frosty?" suggested Jenny. "Yes!" they all cheered.

Marianna said, "I wish Frosty were alive!" Just then, Matt looked up at Frosty's face. "Frosty just winked at me!" he cried.

They all looked up just in time to see Frosty smile. He really was alive! They gave him a big hug. "Hey! I'm ticklish!" he said.

They all laughed, and Frosty began to do a little dance. Suddenly, there was a parade going all around the park, with Frosty leading the way.

Next, Frosty and the children decided to go sledding. They pulled their sleds to the top of the hill and got ready to race. "Oh, no!" said Matt. "Frosty is too big to fit on any of our sleds."

"Don't worry about that," laughed Frosty. "Remember, I'm made of snow. All I have to do is lie down and slide. Watch!" Frosty was right. He could slide as fast as the fastest sled. What a race they all had!

That night, Jenny, Matt, and Marianna could hardly wait to tell their parents about Frosty. "A snowman who talks, dances, and sleds?" said their father. "That's something I'd have to see to believe."

The next morning, the three children borrowed their father's ice skates. Then they ran to find Frosty and their other friends. "Wait until you try ice skating, Frosty," said Lisa. "It's even more fun than sledding."

Frosty bravely put on the skates. "Hey, this isn't so hard!" he called. He learned to skate in a figure eight and even to lift one foot high in the air. "Wheee!" he shouted, tipping his top hat as he whizzed by.

After a while, the children went into the warming house to warm up a bit. But they had forgotten something important. Frosty was made of snow! "Whew! This place doesn't feel so good to me," he said. "I'll wait outside."

While Frosty waited for his friends outside, he noticed one little boy skating near a sign that said, "Danger! Thin ice." Frosty called, "Hey, watch out!" But the boy didn't hear.

Quick as a wink, Frosty darted out onto the ice after the little boy. Just as the ice started to crack, Frosty caught him by the hand and pulled him to safety.

Frosty was a hero! All the children cheered for their friend.

The next day it rained. Matt, Jenny, and Marianna worried about Frosty all day. Finally, the rain stopped. They went out to the park with their father.

They found Frosty's hat next to a little lump of snow. Frosty was gone!

Marianna picked up the hat sadly. And there, underneath it, was a purple flower, the color of Frosty's scarf. "Look," their father said, "he left a promise that he'll be back next year."